In the army

Story by Beth Johnson
Illustrations by Mark Weber

Dr. Judith Nadell, Series Editor

Last week, Derek's friend Brandon

came over to play.

Grandpa made room for the boys to play.

Grandma gave them milk and cookies.

Brandon liked Derek's grandparents a lot.

But he had a question.

"Why do you live with your grandparents?"

Brandon asked.

"Where is your mom?"

"My mom is away at her job," said Derek.

"She is in the army."

"What does she do in the army?"

Brandon asked.

"She does lots of things," Derek said.

"She reads books, does homework,

and uses a computer."

"She runs, jumps, and climbs over walls.

She is really strong and really fast."

"She fixes engines.

She even jumps out of planes!"

"Do you miss your mom?" Brandon asked.

"I miss her a lot," Derek said.

"But she writes every week.

I write to her, too.

I sent her a teddy bear.

She really liked it."

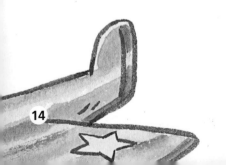

"When she got the teddy bear, she sent me this picture."

"Wow!" said Brandon.